EDDYCAT
Introduces...
Mannersville

For a free color catalog describing Gareth Stevens's list of high-quality books, call 1-800-341-3569 (USA) or 1-800-461-9120 (Canada).

Library of Congress Cataloging-in-Publication Data

Barnett, Ada.
    Eddycat introduces Mannersville / by Ada Barnett, Pam Manquen, and Linda Rapaport : illustrated by Mark Hoffmann.
        p. cm. -- (Social skill builders for children)
    Includes bibliographical references.
    Includes index.
    Summary: When Buddy Brownbear moves to Mannersville, he finds the entire town full of friendly, polite animals who know how to behave properly. At various intervals in the text, Eddycat makes additional comments about etiquette.
    ISBN 0-8368-0939-4
        [1. Etiquette--Fiction. 2. Animals--Fiction.] I. Manquen, Pam. II. Rapaport, Linda. III. Hoffmann, Mark. ill. IV. Title. V. Series
    PZ7.B2629Ee 1993
    [E]--dc20
                                                                                                    92-56877

Published by
Gareth Stevens Publishing
1555 North RiverCenter Drive, Suite 201
Milwaukee, Wisconsin 53212, USA

This edition of *Eddycat Introduces. . . Mannersville* was first published in the USA and Canada by Gareth Stevens, Inc., in association with The Children's Etiquette Institute. Text, artwork, characters, design, and format © 1993 by The Children's Etiquette Institute.

Sincere thanks to educators Jody Henderson-Sykes of Grand Avenue Middle School in Milwaukee, Wisconsin, and Mel Ciena of the University of San Francisco for their invaluable help.

EDDYCAT, EddieCat, and the EDDYCAT symbol and Social Skills for Children are trademarks and service marks of the American Etiquette Institute.

Printed in the United States of America

1 2 3 4 5 6 7 8 9 98 97 96 95 94 93

EDDYCAT
Introduces...
Mannersville

Gareth Stevens Publishing
MILWAUKEE

CONTENTS

Introduction. 5

Eddycat Introduces. . . Mannersville. 6

Eddycat's Helpful Terms 29

More Books to Read 30

Place to Write 30

Parent/Teacher Guide 31

Index. 32

Hi, friends! I'm Eddycat, and I live in a city named Mannersville.

Everyone here believes there is something special about certain words and sentences because they make others smile and feel good.

My goal is to try to make the world a better place in which to live, but I need your help. What you need to do is let others know that you care about them and that you care about yourself. I will show you the special way of doing this. And it will make me very happy to cheer you on as you learn to say the special words and follow the special rules!

Today, I am going to introduce you to my friends here in Mannersville. I hope they will become your friends, too. If you pay close attention, you will learn how to introduce yourself and your friends to others.

Here are some of the special phrases and magical words used in this Eddycat story. Can **you** find these words and sentences in the story?

Please.   *Excuse me.*
Thank you.   *How do you do?*
You're welcome.   *It was nice meeting you.*

This is Mr. and Mrs. Smithbear with their daughter, Sunshine, and their son, Seymour.

They live on First Street in Mannersville.

Sunshine attends Wright Street School. This is
Sunshine's teacher, Ms. Hooten.

Sunshine has many friends. Some of them have unusual names from around the world. It's fun to have friends from different cultures.

But they all have one thing in common... they are all polite!

Becky Bunny likes to climb trees and play on the bars. She also likes making things out of sand or mud.

She sometimes gets very, very dirty!

Buster Bull is a good friend. He always cheers Sunshine along!

Harry Hound likes to flop his ears over his eyes to be funny. He makes Sunshine and the other animals laugh.

But he never makes *fun* of others. He does not want to hurt their feelings.

Danny Duck likes to read. He sometimes reads to his sister, Clara Duck. Clara likes to make up songs and sing to her friends.

Clara also likes to share listening to her radio with her friends.

Rhonda Rabbit doesn't like to join in games that will make her dirty. She likes always to have clean hands, a clean face, and clean clothes.

It's all right if others do not want to join in.

It's been great to meet Sunshine's friends.

Sunshine likes to make *new* friends, too!

This is the Brownbear family. They are new in town. They are just moving into their house on Fourth Street in Mannersville. Mr. and Mrs. Brownbear have a son, Buddy. Their daughter's name is Honey.

Buddy Brownbear is just about Sunshine's age.

Do you think Buddy and Sunshine will be friends?

I do!

Buddy and Sunshine first meet early one morning before school. "Hello, my name is Buddy Brownbear. I am starting school today," says Buddy.

"Hello, my name is Sunshine Smithbear.
Everyone is very friendly here in Mannersville.
Would you like to meet some of my friends?"
asks Sunshine.

I'm proud of you, Sunshine. It is fun to introduce others and make new friends.

"Yes, thank you, that would be very nice!"
says Buddy.

Buddy remembered the special words, "Thank you."

Sunshine says, "Becky, this is Buddy Brownbear. He is starting school today."

"Buddy, this is Becky Bunny. Becky lives in the apartment building across the street from me," says Sunshine.

When making introductions, say the girl's name first to get her attention.

"How do you do, Buddy Brownbear?"
asks Becky with a big smile.

"How do you do, Becky Bunny?" asks
Buddy, smiling.

"I'm taking Buddy to meet some of the others in our class. Would you like to come with us, Becky?" asks Sunshine.

"No, I have to wait here for my father. I forgot my lunch, and he is bringing it to me. But thank you for asking," replies Becky.

Good for you, Sunshine. You invited Becky, and she does not feel left out.

"See you later, Becky," says Sunshine.

"It was nice meeting you, Becky," says Buddy.

"Thank you, Buddy. It was nice meeting you, too," says Becky. Then Sunshine and Buddy walk off to meet the others.

"Excuse me, I would like all of you to meet Buddy Brownbear. He is new to Mannersville, and he lives on Fourth Street.

"Buddy, this is Clara Duck and her brother, Danny. They also live on Fourth Street.

"And this is Harry Hound and Buster Bull," says Sunshine.

"Would you like to join us, Buddy?" asks Danny. "Clara is the scorekeeper of our game, but we need someone to add up the points when we are done."

It's great that you asked Buddy to join in somehow.

"Thanks for asking, but Sunshine has offered to take me to school and introduce me to my new teacher, Ms. Hooten.

"It was nice meeting all of you. Maybe I can play with you tomorrow!" exclaims Buddy.

Buddy, that was very nice of you to thank them. I'm sure they will want to play with you anytime!

"Excuse me, Ms. Hooten. I would like to introduce Buddy Brownbear. He just moved to Mannersville, and he will be in our class," says Sunshine.

"Buddy, this is Ms. Hooten, our teacher," says Sunshine.

"How do you do?" asks Buddy.

"Hello, Buddy. Welcome to Wright Street School.
I'm looking forward to having you in my class,"
says Ms. Hooten.

"I think I am going to like being here at Wright
Street School. I feel very welcome because of
Sunshine and her friends," says Buddy.

As Buddy and Sunshine turn to leave, Buddy holds the door open for Sunshine. "Thank you," says Sunshine.

"You're welcome," says Buddy.

The bears know that when someone holds a door open for them, they should say, "Thank you."

"Buddy, how was your first day at school?
Did you make any new friends?" asks
Mother Brownbear.

"Yes, Mother. I made many new friends at school
today," answers Buddy. "I think I'm going to like
it here in Mannersville."

EDDYCAT'S HELPFUL TERMS

cleanliness
Being sure that you are clean and neatly dressed.

etiquette
The special rules for how to behave and treat others.

"How do you do?"
A polite way to respond when you are introduced.

interrupting
Cutting in on someone else's conversation.

introduction
The act of telling the names of people to each other.

manners
Special words and rules used by people that make everyone involved feel more comfortable.

"Please."
A word used to politely request something.

sharing
Making sure that everyone gets to take part.

"Thank you."
A polite way to let someone know that you appreciate something he or she has given you or done for you.

"You're welcome."
A polite way to respond when someone thanks you.

MORE BOOKS TO READ

The *Eddycat* series is the only truly authoritative collection on etiquette written for children. Nonetheless, the additional titles by other authors listed here represent good support for the concept that courtesy and manners are valuable skills and habits.

Nonfiction:
Eddycat and Buddy Entertain a Guest. Barnett, Manquen, Rapaport (Gareth Stevens)
Eddycat Attends Sunshine's Birthday Party. Barnett, Manquen, Rapaport (Gareth Stevens)
Eddycat Goes Shopping with Becky Bunny. Barnett, Manquen, Rapaport (Gareth Stevens)
Eddycat Helps Sunshine Plan Her Party. Barnett, Manquen, Rapaport (Gareth Stevens)
Eddycat Teaches Telephone Skills. Barnett, Manquen, Rapaport (Gareth Stevens)

I Can Read About Good Manners. Frost (Troll)
Manners: Don't Leave Home Without Them. Jordan (Standard)
May I? Riehecky (Child's World)
Mind Your Manners. Parish (Greenwillow)

Fiction:
Act Nicely, Please. Stause (Abbey)
Lamb Chop in the Land of No Manners. Lewis (Lynx Books)
Monkeys Never Say Please. Davidson (Gibson)

PLACE TO WRITE

For more information about etiquette, contact the American Etiquette Institute, P.O. Box 700508, San Jose, CA 95170.

PARENT/TEACHER GUIDE

appearance   pages 9, 13

There is a time and place for everything. Caring how you look shows consideration for others as well as for yourself. What is appropriate is the key. It would not be appropriate to wear party clothes to clean the garage, and it would not be appropriate to wear work clothes to a party.

doors   page 26

1. In social situations, a male should open and hold a door for a female.
2. A young person, male or female, should open and hold a door for an adult.
3. A host or hostess should hold the door for guests.
4. With friends of the same sex, the person who opens the door should hold it for the other person. It is never correct to barge through a door ahead of others.

introductions – general   pages 16, 17, 22

Knowing how and when to introduce yourself and others is an integral part of good manners. When introducing yourself, always say your first and last name. If you pause slightly between your first and last name, it will help others remember your name.

introductions – social   pages 18, 24

Begin social introductions by:
1. Introducing a male to a female. Say the female's name first to get her attention.
2. Introducing an adult to a much older adult of the same sex.
3. Introducing the lower rank to the higher rank.

4. Introducing children to adults.

Special rules: Smile during all introductions. Boys and girls should stand for ALL introductions. Children should always address adults by their last name (such as Ms. Hooten) unless the adults ask to be addressed by their first name.

responses to social introductions   pages 19, 25

"How do you do?" is the appropriate response under all circumstances. "How do you do, Ms. Hooten?" is the best form. It implies that the other person is important, and it also helps us remember the name. "Hello" or "Hi" are accepted under limited circumstances.

title – Ms.   page 7

Ms. is the accepted title for a businesswoman. A female teacher or other adult will tell the child if she prefers Miss or Mrs. rather than Ms.

INDEX

classroom 24, 25, 26
cleanliness 9, 13

encouragement 10

feelings 11, 20
friends 8, 10, 12, 14, 15,
   22, 25, 27

interrupting 22
introductions 16-18, 22, 24

names 16

requests 20
responding 19, 25

sharing 12

taking turns 14

46

E
B

Barnett, Ada

Eddycat introduces
Mannersville

DATE DUE	BORROWER	
10/21/96	Nancy Barron	46
11-15-96	Jak Le	46

E
B

Barnett, Ada

Eddycat introduces
Mannersville

Anderson Elementary